THE THREE LITTLE PIGS
REIMAGINED!

BY

Jerry Popowich
& Doug Sinclair

ILLUSTRATED BY

Maria Kiriakova

INSTRUCTIONS

1

DOWNLOAD THE FREE MOBILE APP!

Scan the QR code or visit www.incredebooks.com/apps. Look for the The Three Little Pigs - Reimagined app and download the app on your iOS or Android device.

2

READ, THEN LOOK FOR SPECIAL PAGES!

Read the book and look for this symbol on special pages. The are four pages that contain special 3D games!

3

WATCH THE PAGES COME TO LIFE IN 3D!

Launch the app and hold your smart phone or tablet facing the book page that contains the symbol. Make sure the entire page is visible. Now watch the page come to life in 3D!

FIND OUT MORE INFORMATION AT WWW.INCREDEBOOKS.COM

1

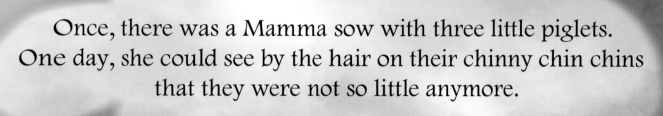

Once, there was a Mamma sow with three little piglets. One day, she could see by the hair on their chinny chin chins that they were not so little anymore.

2

So, she sent them out to find their place in the world.

24

Along the road, the first pig bought
a bundle of straw to build a house.
His brothers laughed at him.

"Silly little pig," they said.
"Someone could huff and puff and blow that house in,"
but he was pretty sure that wouldn't happen.

So, off they went
leaving their brother to build
his house of straw.

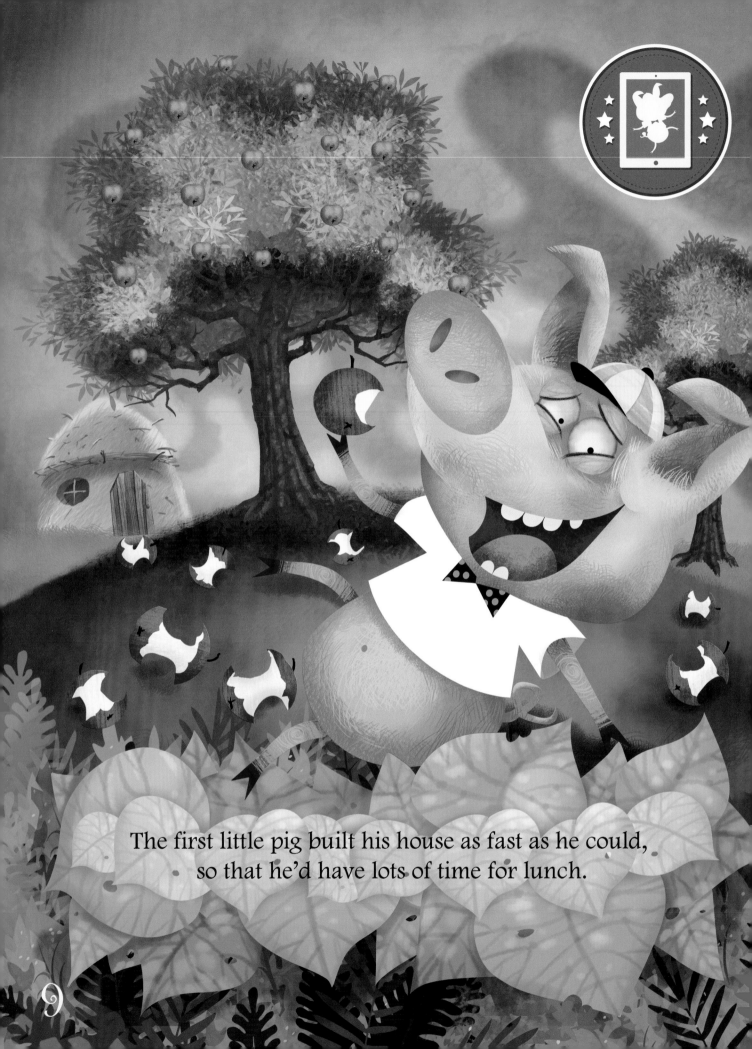

The first little pig built his house as fast as he could,
so that he'd have lots of time for lunch.

And he ate his lunch as fast as he could,
so that he'd have lots of time for a nap.
Napping is much easier than building a house, you know.
You don't even need your eyes open.

A hungry wolf arrived at the little pig's house and growled,
"Little pig, little pig, let me come in!"

"Zzzz…not by the hair on my…
zzzz…chinny chin… zzz…chin…"

So, the wolf huffed...and he puffed...
and he blew the house in! For some reason,
the little pig was surprised.

Frightened, the little pig ran down the road
to his brother's house made of sticks.

The second little pig had also built his house as fast as he could so that he'd have plenty of time to scratch his back. Scratching your back is much easier than building a house, you know! And a whole lot less itchy!

Soon, the hungry wolf arrived at the stick house and growled, "Little pigs, little pigs, let me… oh, never mind. We've done all that."

And he huffed…and he puffed…

19

…and he blew that house in!

The two little pigs ran down the road to their brother's house.

The third little pig had spent all day building
his house out of the finest, strongest bricks.
He was tired from the work,
and his back hadn't been scratched in hours,
but it was worth it.

Soon enough, the wolf arrived at the brick house. "You know what I'm going to say," he said, "and you know what I'm going to do!"

And the wolf huffed…and he puffed.
And he huff puffed…and he puff huffed.
And he puffing huffa puffed.
And he even huffing puff huffo puffy huffed,
and you know how dangerous that can be.

He kept trying until his huffer was all out of puff,
but he could not blow that house in.

24

The little pigs felt badly for him.
"We'll make you a deal," they said.
"If you're so hungry, we'll cook a tasty
vegetable lasagna for you."

This sounded nice to the wolf,
because eating vegetable lasagna
is much easier than blowing houses in.

"What do I have to do in return?" asked the wolf.

26

And they all lived happily ever after.

The End